MARGIT: BOOK TWO

A BIT OF LOVE
AND A BIT OF LUCK

KATHY KACER

Enjoy reading

Kathy Kacer

MARGIT: BOOK TWO

A BIT OF LOVE
AND A BIT OF LUCK

KATHY KACER

PENGUIN
CANADA

PENGUIN CANADA

Published by the Penguin Group

Penguin Group (Canada), 10 Alcorn Avenue, Toronto, Ontario, Canada M4V 3B2
(a division of Pearson Penguin Canada Inc.)

Penguin Group (USA) Inc., 375 Hudson Street, New York, New York 10014, U.S.A.
Penguin Books Ltd, 80 Strand, London WC2R 0RL, England
Penguin Ireland, 25 St Stephen's Green, Dublin 2, Ireland (a division of Penguin Books Ltd)
Penguin Group (Australia), 250 Camberwell Road, Camberwell, Victoria 3124, Australia
(a division of Pearson Australia Group Pty Ltd)
Penguin Books India Pvt Ltd, 11 Community Centre, Panchsheel Park, New Delhi – 110 017, India
Penguin Group (NZ), cnr Airborne and Rosedale Roads, Albany, Auckland 1310, New Zealand
(a division of Pearson New Zealand Ltd)
Penguin Books (South Africa) (Pty) Ltd, 24 Sturdee Avenue, Rosebank, Johannesburg 2196,
South Africa

Penguin Books Ltd, Registered Offices: 80 Strand, London WC2R 0RL, England

First published 2005

1 2 3 4 5 6 7 8 9 10   (WEB)

Copyright © Kathy Kacer, 2005
Cover and interior illustrations copyright © Janet Wilson, 2005
Design: Matthews Communications Design Inc.
Map copyright © Sharon Matthews

Lyrics on page 29 from a loose translation of the folk song "I Have a Horse" by Antonin Dvorak.

Lyrics on page 80 from a loose translation of the folk song "Spring" by Friedrich Holderlin.

Manufactured in Canada.

LIBRARY AND ARCHIVES CANADA CATALOGUING IN PUBLICATION

Kacer, Kathy, 1954–
Margit : a bit of love and a bit of luck / Kathy Kacer.

(Our Canadian girl)
"Margit: Book Two".
ISBN 0-14-301675-X

1. Refugees, Jewish—Ontario—Toronto—Juvenile fiction.
I. Title. II. Title: Bit of love and a bit of luck. III. Series.

PS8571.A33M36 2005   jC813'.54   C2004-905414-7

Visit the Penguin Group (Canada) website at **www.penguin.ca**

For Lisa Dennill,
my wonderful niece and best fan

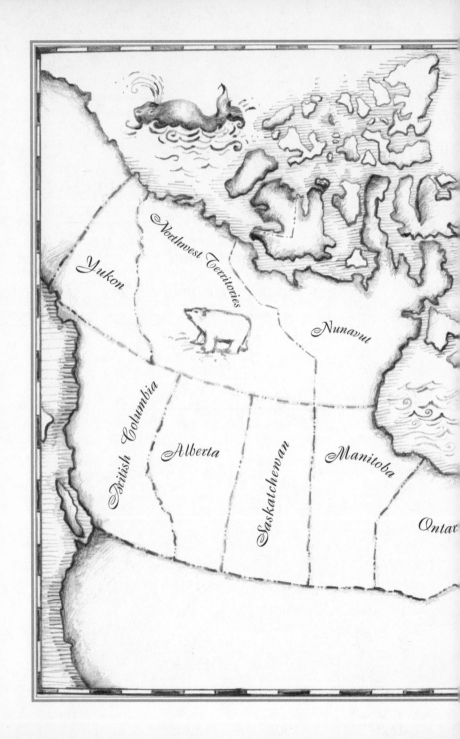

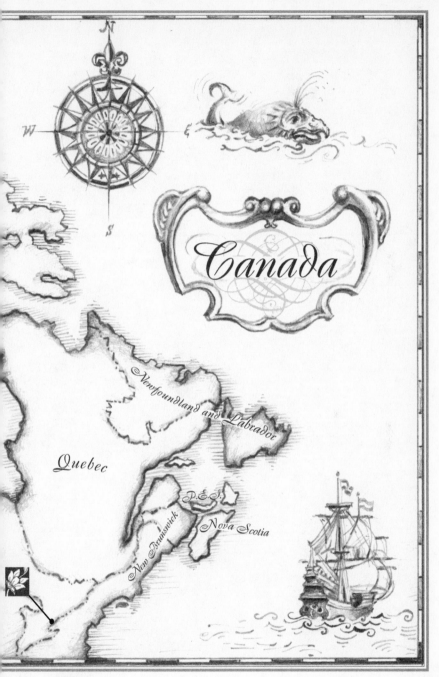

Canada

Newfoundland and Labrador

Quebec

P.E.I.

New Brunswick

Nova Scotia

 Marks the location of the story

REUNITED

It is January 1946, and World War II has been over for more than eight months. Twelve-year-old Margit Freed has been living in Canada for a year and a half, having fled from her homeland of Czechoslovakia. Her father was left behind, imprisoned in one of the many concentration camps of Europe.

With the war's end, more and more information has been trickling out of Europe about the treatment of Jews at the hand of Adolf Hitler and his evil Nazi Party. More than six million Jewish people were killed during the war, most of them in concentration camps. Margit's father was among the lucky ones who survived. But it hasn't been easy getting him to Canada. Canada is still not eager to open its doors to strangers, especially Jews. The government of Prime Minister Mackenzie King still fears that Canada is in danger of being flooded with Jewish people. And without the abundance brought by wartime spending, there are dire predictions that Canada will slip back into a depression. Businesses will suffer and jobs will disappear.

Margit and her mother have worked hard to overcome the obstacles, and Margit is filled with anticipation and joy that her family will soon be reunited with her Papa. But even as Margit is thrilled about seeing her father, she is also anxious. Will Papa even recognize her after all this time? And will she know him? Now that Margit is struggling in one of her classes at school, will she ever measure up to his expectations?

CHAPTER N° 1

"Margit, I need to speak with you." The teacher held up a single sheet of paper as her gaze settled on twelve-year-old Margit Freed.

Margit looked up from the book she was reading and gulped. She brushed her curly brown bangs away from her face. "Yes, Mrs. Cook?"

Silence blanketed the classroom. Mrs. Cook hesitated. She looked troubled. "Perhaps you could come up to my desk," she said. "That way we can have a more private conversation."

All eyes were on Margit as she rose from her seat. She glanced at Alice, her best friend since

Margit had arrived in Toronto a year and a half earlier from Czechoslovakia. Alice smiled encouragingly as Margit made her way past the rows of desks to face Mrs. Cook at the front of the classroom.

"Margit, I'm very concerned about your grades in science. You don't seem to understand this work at all." Mrs. Cook peered out severely over dark-rimmed glasses. As she held out the test sheet, Margit's eyes zeroed in on the grade at the top. The D was written in red, underlined, and circled. It stood out on the page, glowing like a warning light on a dark night. "Have you spoken to your mother about my concerns? I asked you to have her call me, but so far I haven't heard from her."

"I ... I tried to talk to her, Mrs. Cook, but ... you see ... you know ... well ..."

Mrs. Cook waved her hand impatiently. "No excuses, Margit. Your schoolwork is too important to neglect. I know it has taken some time for you to learn English, and I've been patient with you about that. But I must speak with your mother so that we can make a plan to deal with this problem."

Margit shifted from one foot to the other, squirming under Mrs. Cook's piercing stare. "But you see, Mrs. Cook, my father is arriving tomorrow, and we haven't seen him in so long, and my mother has been so busy, and ..."

"There are just too many 'ands' and 'buts,' Margit. Here." Mrs. Cook held the paper out to Margit, who reluctantly accepted it. "I've added another note for your mother to call me. She will call, won't she, Margit?"

Margit sighed deeply as the school bell rang and students all around her rushed for the door. Mrs. Cook called out to her class. "Don't forget that your history projects are due tomorrow."

Margit used the opportunity to slink back to her seat. She gathered her books, folded the test, and shoved it deep into her schoolbag. She quickly grabbed her heavy winter coat and headed out the door with Alice at her side. The girls ran down the steps of the school, under the banner that read Lord Lansdowne Public School. Together, they crossed Spadina Avenue and set off toward the market. Schoolchildren rushed past them, eager to get home. Mothers pushed babies in carriages that also held shopping bags filled with groceries for that evening's supper. Drivers swerved through traffic after a long day at work, skidding dangerously on the slippery roads. Margit pulled up her coat collar, bracing against the icy wind.

"Mrs. Cook is so strict," said Alice. "And she's the hardest marker I've ever had."

Margit smiled gratefully. Alice was always trying to make her feel better. "It's not that, Alice. Mrs. Cook is right. I don't understand this work in science. Math is fine. It's probably my best subject. I even do okay in English, even though my grammar isn't always that good. But all those scientific words and definitions are just so confusing to me."

"What did your mother say when you told her to call the teacher?"

"That's just it, Alice. I haven't told her. And I can't. She wouldn't understand. It's too important for her that I do well in school."

Alice nodded. "It's important for my parents as well."

"Yes, but it's different for me—for my family. Jewish children like me couldn't even go to school when the war started in Czechoslovakia. So now that the war is over and we're living in a free country, an education is one of the most important things we can have."

It was still hard at times to explain these things to Alice. Of course education was important to Alice and her parents too. But to Margit's family, it was a lifeline. "In Canada, no one will stop you from getting a good education, Margit," Mamma always said. "And when you are in school in Toronto, you will do better than anyone else. You're smart and you will do great things." Those words echoed in Margit's head. Mamma would never understand a D in science.

Margit said goodbye to Alice and turned up the

snowy walkway to her apartment. School and the problems she was having in science would have to wait. More important things were happening in Margit's home. Papa was arriving.

CHAPTER N.º 2

"When will Papa ever get here?" Margit asked anxiously, straining to peer over the crowd of people gathered at the train station. The building took up one entire block on Front Street, and it was full of families waiting for loved ones to arrive. Light poured into the great hall from the four-storey-tall windows at either end of the massive arched ceiling. Margit spoke in Czech, as she and Mamma always did together. Czech was the language of their homeland.

"Soon, darling. He'll be here soon. We must be patient." The look on Mamma's face was anything but patient, thought Margit. Mamma looked nervous and jumpy. But there was also something else that Margit could sense from Mamma—something Margit had not seen for a long time. Mamma was excited. Her family was finally going to be reunited.

The train due to arrive at Union Station was carrying Margit's father, Leo Freed. Margit closed her eyes and thought back to the last time she had seen Papa, a year and half earlier. That was so long ago! They were still in Czechoslovakia, and World War II was still raging. So many Jewish people had been arrested and even killed by the Nazis, the army of the evil Adolf Hitler. Margit knew that Papa had been held in a concentration camp—one of many prisons in which millions of Jews had been starved, tortured, and often killed.

Mamma and Margit had been among the lucky ones, able to escape and make their way to Canada. But escaping had meant leaving Papa behind, and for a full year after their arrival in Toronto, Margit and her mother were tormented with worries about Papa's safety. The letter that arrived in June 1945, announcing that he was alive and coming to join them, had brought immediate joy to their lives.

Jack squirmed restlessly in Mamma's arms. He hated being held for so long. "Margit, would you please hold your brother for a few minutes?" Mamma asked. "I'm going to find someone who can give me information about when the train might arrive."

Margit reached out her arms to her one-year-old baby brother as Mamma disappeared into the crowd. Jack wrapped his chubby arms around his sister's neck and snuggled happily into her arms. But that only lasted a moment.

"Dow …," whined Jack, pushing and kicking his arms and legs against Margit's grasp.

"I can't put you down, Jack. You'll get lost with all these people here." Jack continued to wiggle around as Margit tried bouncing her brother up and down. "Calm down, Jack. We're going to see Papa soon. Don't you want to see Papa?"

Jack paused and looked into Margit's face. He wrapped his fingers in her long brown curly hair and tugged gently. "Ma ... ma?"

Margit laughed and rubbed her nose into Jack's soft belly. "Not Mamma, silly. We're here to meet Papa. Can you say 'Pa ... pa'?"

Jack scrunched up his nose and pressed his lips together. "Ba ...ba."

Margit sighed. "Well, I guess that's close enough for now." Briefly, she wondered what this first meeting between father and son was going to be like. But she wondered even more about her own reunion with her father. Would he look and act different? Would she even recognize him? And would he know her? After all, Margit had changed so much since coming to Canada. She was twelve years old now, taller, and more grown up. She spoke English with only a slight European accent. She even looked like a Canadian girl, dressed in a blue pleated skirt and white blouse that Mamma had sewn just for this occasion. Everything about Margit looked and

Jack wrapped his chubby arms around his sister's neck and snuggled happily into her arms.

felt different. She had worked hard every day to fit in, to make friends, and to learn new things.

Margit cringed slightly, remembering the science test she had hidden away in her room without showing Mamma. Yes, the adjustment to this country had been hard at times for Margit. But how could it begin to compare with the suffering Papa had experienced at the hands of the Nazis?

In recent months, there had been more information about the millions of Jews who had died or been killed during the war—so many more than anyone had ever imagined. Margit had watched a newsreel at the movie theatre that showed the freeing of a concentration camp in Europe, like the one where Papa had been imprisoned. Starved, ghost-like people stared back from the screen, wasted and barely alive. She couldn't watch, it terrified her so.

"They say it will be only be ten more minutes until the train arrives." Mamma reappeared in the crowd and reached over for Jack. She dug into

her bag and pulled out a cookie. Jack smiled and
grabbed the treat, shoving it happily into his
mouth. "Ba ... ba," he said, through a mouthful
of crumbs.

"He's trying to say 'Papa,'" said Margit.

"Ba ... ba," Jack repeated, as Mamma gently
stroked his cheek.

"Yes, my baby boy," said Mamma. "You'll see
your Papa soon. And you too, Margit," she added.
"Oh, we've all waited so long for this day."

It had not been easy getting Papa here. After
the war ended, Canada had not been eager to
open its doors to immigrants—newcomers from
foreign countries. So, even though Margit knew
that Papa was alive and safe, he still seemed
unreachable. He might as well have been living
on another planet, Margit thought. That's how
far away he felt.

With Margit's help, Mamma had written
dozens of letters to the Canadian government,
begging for the documents necessary for Papa to
be admitted into Canada. Many thousands of

people were refused entry. It was nothing short of a miracle when permission arrived, months later. Then there was the problem of raising enough money to send to Papa for the boat and train tickets that would bring him here—money that Mamma did not have. The Jewish Immigrant Aid Society had helped. The organization was working desperately to rescue Jewish refugees from Europe. And members of Margit's synagogue had been kind and generous. Slowly but surely, Mamma had put aside small amounts of money, spending less and less on clothing and food, until finally all was in order—the papers, the tickets, and the date when Papa was set to arrive: January 10, 1946.

"NOW ARRIVING ON PLATFORM B, THE 6:00 P.M. TRAIN FROM HALIFAX." The announcement boomed on the loudspeakers. "PLEASE PROCEED TO THE ARRIVALS AREA TO MEET YOUR PARTIES."

Margit inhaled sharply and looked at Mamma.

CHAPTER N° 3

Suddenly, there he was. Papa stepped off the train onto the platform and looked over at the family that was waiting for him. Without a moment's hesitation, he stumbled forward and reached out for Mamma first, wrapping his arms around her in a tender, loving hug. Margit watched shyly. It almost embarrassed her to see her parents embrace in this way. Jack wriggled and squirmed as his mother held him, struggling to push away the arms that Papa had wrapped around his small frame as well. Jack looked so confused. He stared at Papa, frowned, and then looked over at Margit. Who was this stranger grabbing him like this?

Mamma finally pulled away and held up Jack for Papa to see. "Leo, this is your son," she said through flowing tears. "This is Jack. He's named for Yacov, my late father."

Papa hesitated a moment, and then he reached out to stroke Jack's round cheek. Jack started to push Papa's hand away and then paused. He grabbed Papa's finger and shoved it into his mouth, sucking and chewing noisily as if he had been given a new toy or a delicious treat.

Papa smiled a sad and happy smile. "He's beautiful—a strong boy. And born here, right? Born in Canada?"

"Yes," said Mamma. "He was born here in Toronto."

"That's good," replied Papa. "It's good to be born in a free country."

Margit looked on, a bit anxious at first, watching the exchange between her father and her brother. Everything about Papa seemed different.

He looked small and pale, thinner than Margit remembered. His once strong frame seemed to have shrivelled, and his clothes hung on his frail body. Even his hair was different. Papa had once had a full head of thick brown hair, just like the curls she herself had inherited. Margit recalled the mornings she had watched Papa comb his hair carefully to one side, applying the hair lotion that held it neatly in place. Now, that beautiful curly hair was gone, replaced with grey clumps that sprouted in irregular places around his head. Papa was stooped and walked with a slight limp that had never been there before. Margit wondered where that had come from.

In fact, she wondered about all the things that had happened to Papa in the last year and a half. Had he been beaten, or starved? Had he seen other Jews die while he had somehow managed to stay alive in the concentration camp? And how had he survived? All these questions swirled in Margit's mind as she looked at her father.

Papa eased his hand from Jack's grasp and finally

turned in her direction. "No," he said, gasping in surprise. "This can't be my beautiful Margit! Why, you were just a child when I last saw you. And now … well, this is a young woman." He held out his thin arms and Margit rushed headlong into his grasp. She worried she might throw him off his feet with her weight. But Papa wobbled only a little and he hugged her tightly, as if he never wanted to let go again. Margit inhaled, searching desperately for a smell—anything that might remind her of her father. Where was the scent of that hair lotion, or the musty odour of his business suit, smells that would tell Margit at once that this was the father she had left behind in Europe? They were nowhere to be found in this weakened man.

"Papa," she murmured through her tears. "I'm so glad you're here." There was so much more she wanted to say.

"Me too, my Margitka," he whispered, using the name only he called her. "Me too."

Mamma looked on with tears glistening in her eyes, while Jack just stared and frowned.

Margit was afraid to let go of her father, afraid that he might disappear again if she loosened her hold. So, she just hugged and hugged with all her might. It felt as if many minutes had passed before she finally stepped back and looked into her father's eyes. They were more hollow than she remembered and certainly sadder, as if they held a truth about his suffering that was too painful to speak about. But deep inside, Margit saw the glimmer of her father's old self, his kindness and his strength. He had survived the war, and she could see the determination behind the sorrow.

"You must be exhausted," said Mamma, taking charge. "And hungry. You're so thin, Leo. You've wasted away."

Papa nodded. "You always worried too much about my eating," he said, affectionately. "But you're right. I am tired and ready to go home with my family."

Home, thought Margit. *They were going home together.*

CHAPTER No 4

Papa said little on the streetcar ride back to the apartment, while Margit kept up a steady stream of chatter, pointing out the sights of Toronto. "Down there is Alice's house, Papa. She's my best friend. Her parents work in Kensington Market. They have a flower shop and Alice helps them after school. I've helped there too." Margit clutched her father's hand as she spoke.

"It's good to have a friend, Margitka," Papa replied softly.

"Wait until you see the market, Papa. It will remind you of home—I mean home the way it used to be, before … well, just the way it used to be." Margit stumbled over the words, not wanting to mention the war or what it had done to their homeland, not wanting to cause her father unnecessary pain. "You can buy fish and cheese and vegetables and anything you need. It's all there."

"Stop, Margit," said Mamma sternly. "You're talking too much and your Papa is tired." Mamma's eyes warned Margit to be careful with what she was saying.

"Ba … ba," said Jack, looking at Papa and then back at his mother.

Papa smiled and gently stroked Jack's head. "No," he insisted. "I like to hear Margit talk. It's fine, Miriam. I've waited so long to hear Margit's voice. It gives me strength."

Margit glanced at her mother, who paused before nodding. Then Margit continued. "And that's our synagogue, Papa. It's called the Anshe Minsk synagogue. We go for services on Friday nights. All the people know you're coming, Papa."

Papa nodded. "The synagogues back home are all gone," he said, looking over at Mamma. "They were destroyed by Hitler. It will be good to enter a place of prayer again." It was Papa's first reference to the destruction of Jewish life during the war.

Mamma reached over and touched her husband's arm gently. "We can pray freely here, Leo."

"Yes, Miriam," replied Papa. "Freedom is a good thing." It was the second time Papa had spoken about the importance of freedom.

"And what about school, Margit?" Papa continued, turning back to his daughter. "You haven't said anything yet about school. I want to know all about how my smart girl is doing."

Margit gulped and thought again about her science test. "School is fine," she said.

"Only fine?" replied Papa, sounding troubled.

"Margit is being modest," interrupted Mamma. "She is a wonderful student, with only the very best grades, aren't you, Margit? Tell Papa how well you are doing in school."

"Well, school has been hard," began Margit. "It was very hard to learn English."

"Yes, but she's done so well," said Mamma. "I can barely put an English sentence together, but not Margit. She speaks English as if she were born in Canada—not a trace of the old language at all."

"Sometimes I forget words," Margit continued.

"Not often," said Mamma. "And talk about math, Margit. She is at the top of her class in math, Leo."

Papa nodded. "You see? I knew you were a smart girl."

Margit sighed. Her parents' faces glowed with hope and pride. It meant so much to them that she do well in all her studies, that she succeed. How could she disappoint them by telling them that she was struggling with science? There and then, she resolved not to talk about the science test.

Papa reached over and touched Margit's face. It seemed as if he could not let go of his children either, could not believe that he was actually touching them. "Always remember, Margit," he said, "with a good education you can do anything, go anywhere. No one can take that away from you. Whatever else happens, you must do well in school."

Margit swallowed the lump in her throat and nodded.

By the time Margit and her family arrived at the apartment, it was dark and Papa was exhausted. Margit lead the way upstairs, walking up the narrow staircase, past the tailor shop below. The sewing machines had long since ceased their hum and clatter.

Margit held the door open for Papa, who cautiously entered their home. Mamma followed, still carrying Jack, who by now was slumped in her arms, fast asleep

Margit ran around the tiny apartment, happily pointing out its features to Papa. "We've hung this curtain in the living room, Papa, and my bed is on the other side. I used to sleep with Mamma in that bedroom. But this is even better because it's almost like having my own room.

"And there's the kitchen. And we're really lucky because we even have our own bathroom. All the people down the hall have to share a bathroom with the tailor shop downstairs. Sometimes the line to the bathroom is so long and they end up having to wait until it's almost too late!

"And there's Mamma's sewing machine. That's where she makes the things for the tailor downstairs. He brings her the material and she sews collars, pockets, and other things. And when she's ready, I take the things downstairs to the tailor and he pays me, and I bring the money back up to Mamma …"

Margit's voice trailed off as she suddenly became aware of Papa's silence. "What do you think, Papa?" she asked finally. "Do you like it?"

Papa nodded. "You've done so much here without me," he said sadly. "How have you done it all?"

Margit felt the pangs of guilt. Her father had been left out of such an important time in their lives. Her life had moved forward, while Papa's had been stopped—almost severed.

"We've managed," said Mamma simply. "But now that you're here, the apartment and our lives are complete."

Margit nodded. Mamma always knew the right thing to say.

"And now, I think it's time for your Papa to go to sleep," Mamma continued. "In fact we should all go to sleep. Jack is already there." She indicated the sleeping bundle on her shoulder. "It's been a long day and we are all tired."

"But we have one more surprise for Papa, don't we, Mamma?" cried Margit.

Before her mother could say anything more, Margit flew across the living room, dragging her father after her. "Look, Papa," she said, pointing at the corner of the room. There sat a wooden cabinet. Margit flung open the top to reveal an old record player. "We just got it. We found it in a shop that was going out of business. It's used, but it works perfectly."

Papa's eyes glowed as he reached out to touch the cabinet. "I haven't heard a song on a record player for years," he said. "Margit, do you remember the old phonograph in our house?"

Margit nodded. "And look, Papa. We even have some old records." Margit placed a record carefully on the turntable, turned the knob, and brought the arm down to rest in the record groove. At first, there was only a crackle and soft hiss. Then the music began and melodic Czech voices filled the room.

I have a horse so fine,
He carries me with ease.
Across the hills and valleys,
In the damp morning breeze.

"Ah!" exclaimed Papa. "Where did you find this song?"

"We found a whole bunch of old Yiddish records and Czech songs that you love, Papa. They're all here." Margit held the stack of records out to her father. For the next hour, Papa's weariness was forgotten. Margit sat on the floor while her father played record after record—old songs that recalled a happier time. Margit watched her father as he closed his eyes and hummed along to the records in his deep baritone voice. *How wonderful it is to be together,* she thought. *And soon, Papa will forget everything that has happened in the past and we'll be a regular family just like before. It will be even better now because we have Jack.*

They listened to the music for an hour before Mamma finally came to turn off the record player and urge her family to go to bed. Margit kissed her mother goodnight and then turned to her father, who hugged her tenderly.

"My Margitka," he said. "My beautiful Margitka. *Bist a zeiskite,*" he murmured in

Yiddish, the language he often spoke privately with Mamma. They were the first few words to Papa's favourite song, a song he had sung many times when she was a child. "You're a sweetheart, and you make my life easier. You are as beautiful as the whole world." Margit stood in the complete peacefulness of her father's embrace. Then she watched her parents disappear into the bedroom. She pushed aside the curtain, undressed, and climbed into bed.

Margit lay awake a long time, thinking about the events of the day. She still couldn't believe that Papa was just steps away from her in the next room and that he was going to be there in the morning, the next day, and the one after that. Perhaps tomorrow she would take Papa to the market. She couldn't wait to introduce her father to Alice. Alice had been so excited to introduce her brother to Margit when he returned from the war. He was a young soldier, fighting with the First Canadian Army in Germany. When he returned to Toronto, Alice had shown him off proudly to everyone. Well, now Margit had her father to show off! *Yes,* she thought, as her eyes finally closed, *everything was going to be just perfect.*

CHAPTER №6

The next morning, Margit dressed quietly for school, putting on her wool stockings and warmest sweater. Mamma and Jack were already up and in the kitchen when Margit entered. Jack was playing on the floor, placing pots and pans on top of his head like hats and then knocking on each one, delighting in the sound as it echoed inside his ears.

"Ma … git," he cried when he saw her. Mamma's soup pot was angled comically on Jack's head so that only one eye was showing.

Margit smiled and knelt down to kiss Jack's

soft neck. "You're so silly, Jack," she said as her brother giggled with delight. Margit looked up. "Good morning, Mamma. Where's Papa?" It felt both strange and nice to be asking that question.

"Still sleeping," Mamma replied. "He was troubled last night and had difficulty settling." Mamma shook her head. "The nightmares are bad. I thought at one point he might wake the whole apartment building with his cries."

Margit nodded. During the night, she had awoken to noises coming from the bedroom. It had almost sounded like a hurt animal—a wounded dog that was drowning and struggling to come up for air. She had pulled the covers over her head to shut out the noise. There was so much she wanted to know about what had happened to Papa during the war, and there was so much she didn't want to know—was afraid to know.

After breakfast, Margit struggled into her heavy winter coat, wrapped a hand-knit scarf around her neck, and headed out the door, blowing kisses to Mamma and Jack, who stood watching and waving.

Alice was waiting for Margit when she arrived at school. "So, tell me all about it," said Alice. "How is your father? Was he excited to see you? Was he happy to see Jack?"

Margit nodded over and over. "It's hard to explain, Alice. I mean, it's great having my father here—more than great. But it's also a bit like having a stranger in the house. He's different and we're different."

Margit and Alice continued talking as they entered their classroom and took their seats. The bell had not yet rung and Mrs. Cook was busy at the blackboard, writing a homework assignment for the class. She turned briefly and, seeing Margit, motioned her to come up to the front of the class. Margit gulped. The science test! In the excitement of having her father home, she had managed to put the test out of her mind. Now it fell back into focus all too clearly. Margit felt queasy as she approached the blackboard and Mrs. Cook's stern look.

"Well?" Mrs. Cook had one hand on her hip while the other waved the chalk in front of Margit's nose. "I did not receive a call from your mother, Margit. I don't understand what's going on."

"I'm sorry, Mrs. Cook." Margit's voice sounded small and timid.

"'I'm sorry'? Is that all you have to say?"

"I've been trying to tell you, Mrs. Cook, that this is a bad time for my family. I mean, it's a good time, but it's just that we are very busy. My mother is ... well ... preoccupied because my father has just arrived from Europe."

Mrs. Cook stared harder. "I don't understand, Margit. There is nothing more important than your studies."

Mrs. Cook was beginning to sound like her parents, thought Margit. Margit lowered her head and sighed. "Yes, Mrs. Cook."

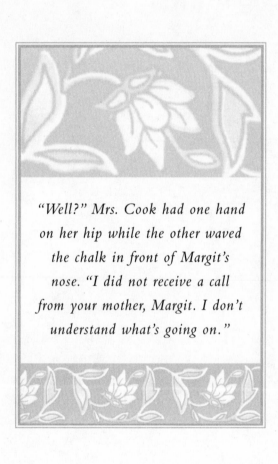

"Well?" Mrs. Cook had one hand on her hip while the other waved the chalk in front of Margit's nose. "I did not receive a call from your mother, Margit. I don't understand what's going on."

"We have another science test coming up in a couple of weeks."

Margit nodded. She knew about the test and was already struggling to learn the material.

"I'll give you one more opportunity to improve your grade," continued Mrs. Cook. "After that, no more chances. If you do poorly on this test, I will pay a visit to your mother myself!"

Margit's head snapped up and she stared at her teacher in dismay.

"I can see that is not something you want, is it?"

Margit shook her head. Other students were beginning to file into the classroom as the bell rang.

"Then make sure you do well." Mrs. Cook dismissed Margit with a wave of her hand.

As she walked back to her desk, Margit's mind was spinning—a mess and mass of confused thoughts. She was already dreading the approaching science test. How could she possibly explain this situation to her parents? And worst of all, how could she prevent Mrs. Cook from showing up on her doorstep?

At recess, Margit made her way out the door and into the playground. Schoolchildren ran in all directions, sliding on icy snowbanks, building snowmen, and making snow angels in the deep fluffy drifts. But not Margit. Not today. Feeling gloomy, she trudged to a small bench at one end of the playground and sat heavily on the seat. Alice joined her a moment later.

"This is terrible," said Margit. "Not only will I fail the test in science, but Mrs. Cook will also come to my house! My parents will be furious with me. What am I going to do?"

Alice gazed at her friend. "Give your parents a chance, Margit. You're acting as if they're going to hate you because of this."

Margit shook her head. "You still don't understand, Alice. If I let them down, I'll ruin everything."

"Just talk to your parents," sighed Alice. "They'll understand."

Margit turned away. She didn't want to have this conversation with Alice any more.

"I'll help you study for this science test, if you want," said Alice.

Margit didn't answer, and Alice finally went off to play with the other children. Margit sat alone until the bell rang again, signalling the end of recess. After school, Margit walked home alone. Alice meant well and Margit didn't mean to turn her back on her best friend. But she needed to figure out this problem by herself.

CHAPTER N.º 7

Margit entered the apartment to find Papa sitting in the deep armchair in the living room, listening to records. Jack played happily on the floor at Papa's feet. *It hadn't been a dream after all,* Margit thought, listening to her father hum the tunes drifting from the record player. Papa really was here. Briefly, she thought back to the conversation with Alice. Maybe Papa would understand if she spoke with him about her struggles in science. Quickly she shook her head. This was not the time to worry him.

"Ah, Margit," cried Papa, delighted to see

his daughter. "Tell me, how was your school today?"

Margit had just opened her mouth when suddenly Mamma appeared from the kitchen, carrying a glass of steaming tea. She set it down beside Papa.

"Margit. You're home. That's good. There's something I'd like you to do for me."

"Yes, Mamma." Saved again, thought Margit.

"I'd like you to go with Papa to the Law Society, Margit. You'll have just enough time to get there before the office closes at six," said Mamma as she watched her husband sip the tea. She had made it with lemon and honey, just the way he used to like it. Papa smiled gratefully at his wife as she continued. "Papa wants to inquire about work. I would go, but I have to finish sewing some skirt hems for the tailor today. Besides, Papa will need your strong English to help with the translation."

"It will be good to get back to work," said Papa. Margit's father had been a lawyer at one of the largest law firms in Prague, the capital city of Czechoslovakia. When the war began, Jewish lawyers like Papa had only been allowed to serve Jewish clients. Eventually, they had lost their positions altogether. That was well before the time that Papa had been arrested and Margit and her mother had fled.

"I haven't stepped inside a courtroom in years," Papa continued.

"There are many law firms that need qualified people like you, Leo," insisted Mamma. She told Margit which streetcar to take and how to get to the Law Society.

Papa finished his tea and rose from the chair to get into the heavy winter coat that Mamma had found for him. He and Margit put on hats and gloves, and then headed out into the cold afternoon air.

Margit walked slowly and carefully. Papa was still weak and his pronounced limp slowed him down considerably. Margit clutched her father's arm and pushed him onto the streetcar. She had to make sure he didn't slip out of her grasp or sight. The downtown core of the city was pulsing with activity, and traffic was thick. Streetcars rumbled along the tracks, followed by honking cars and people darting into and out of traffic. Just past the General Hospital, Margit turned to her father. "We'll get off here and walk to the Law Society."

Margit helped her father off the streetcar and down the street. The Law Society of Upper Canada was located in Osgoode Hall on Queen Street. Margit and her father approached the stately wrought-iron gates of the building and manoeuvred through the twisting entrance. The gate had been built like a tight maze to keep out cows and other animals that had roamed freely when the surrounding area had been farmland.

Together, Margit and Papa entered the majestic rotunda of Osgoode Hall, with its high domed ceiling and marble floor. After inquiring at the information desk, Margit steered her father down the long hallway to the registrar's office.

"Good afternoon," Margit began, when they were finally escorted into the office of a man who introduced himself as Mr. McIntyre. Margit spoke in her most polite voice. "My name is Margit Freed and this is my father, Leo Freed. He has just arrived from Czechoslovakia and is looking for work as a lawyer." Margit went on to explain her father's circumstances, describing how she and her mother had come to Toronto, leaving her father behind, and how he had survived the war to join them.

Mr. McIntyre opened a file and dutifully wrote down everything Margit told him, including their address and phone number.

Periodically, her father would interrupt to add a point or two in Czech. "Tell the gentleman the name of the law firm where I worked," urged Papa. "Tell him I was there for ten years." Margit would nod and then relate the additional pieces of information.

When Margit was finished, Mr. McIntyre sat back, closed the file, and looked intently at Margit and her father. Finally, he pushed his glasses up on his nose and spoke carefully. "I understand your situation and I am sympathetic," he began. "But I am afraid I have bad news for you. Only Canadian citizens are permitted to work as lawyers."

Margit translated quickly and watched her father's face grow pale. "My father intends to stay in Canada and become a citizen as soon as he is allowed," explained Margit.

Mr. McIntyre nodded. "Once again, I am sorry, but tell your father that his plan is simply not good enough. Besides, he only speaks a bit of English. How could he possibly practise law in Canada with no English?"

"I speak much English," Papa said aloud. Margit cringed. Papa knew some English from his own schooling. But his accent was thick, and he suddenly sounded and looked so foreign. "Tell the man I will learn," urged Papa. "Tell him I will be able to work with other immigrants who are new to the country like me. Tell him I speak five other languages. Surely that is good enough."

Mr. McIntyre shook his head as Margit translated. "Your father has no schooling in this country. Our laws are different from European laws. It would take many years of university for your father to become a lawyer here."

"How many years?" asked Papa.

"At least three. Maybe five," was the reply.

Papa's face fell again. "Five years," he murmured under his breath. "How is that possible?"

Mr. McIntyre stood to signal the end of the meeting. He pushed the file to one side of his desk and shook hands with Margit and her father. "Tell your father I am sympathetic. But the law in Canada is firm. If he wishes to resume his law studies, tell your father to come and talk to me again."

CHAPTER N°8

Still holding her father's arm, Margit left Osgoode Hall and walked back through the iron gates. She couldn't bear to look up at Papa, couldn't stand the thought that he might be in pain, frustrated by the news that he would not be able to work as a lawyer. He had suffered so much in these past few years. Margit couldn't accept that he might be suffering again. It was only after they had left the grounds and stopped a block away that Margit gazed tentatively up at her father.

Papa's already tired face looked even more worn out. Deep worry lines creased his forehead and extended down around his eyes. "Five years," he muttered, shaking his head. "How can I wait five years? I must work. We need more money now that I am here. Mamma's income from the tailor shop will not be enough for four."

"Maybe I can help," offered Margit timidly. "I can babysit and earn some extra money. I'm very good with Jack."

Papa's eyes softened and his gaze rested lovingly on Margit's face. "Ah, my Margitka," he said. "Mamma's job is important. But your babysitting money will do little to help us. I must find work. I must find something. I am an educated man. No one will deny that. In Canada there is work!" he said in a determined voice. "I just know it."

Margit and her father turned toward the streetcar stop, bracing against the cold wind. Papa walked with his head down, while Margit searched for something to say. Words failed her.

When they arrived home, Mamma took one look at their faces and didn't even have to ask what had happened. She quickly took charge.

"I'm preparing a feast for you," she said. "We're together, aren't we? Isn't that what is most important?"

"But Miriam," interrupted Papa, "we must talk about what will happen. We must talk about the work."

"There will be work. And we have lots of time to talk about it," continued Mamma. "But tonight, we'll celebrate as a family." Quickly she set to work, finishing the *gulas,* a beef stew with fluffy dumplings smothered in gravy on the side. For dessert, she made special crepes called *palacinky,* filled with jam and drizzled with chocolate. It was the kind of feast Papa had not seen in years. But it did little to lift his spirits.

"Eat," Mamma urged. "We have so much to be grateful for. The Nazis did not defeat us, and this won't either. Our family is together and we're healthy. Even Jack is eating more than you are."

Sure enough, Jack was busy shovelling handfuls of dessert into his mouth. At the sound of his name, he looked up at Margit and grinned. It looked to Margit as if there was more food on Jack's face, hair, and clothing than in his mouth. "Good," said Jack, making a smacking sound with his lips.

Papa looked sadly at his son. *"A bis'l libe un a bisele glick,"* said Papa. "A little bit of love and a little bit of luck. We have the love and now all we need is the luck." He turned quickly to Margit. "You and Jack are so lucky, my Margitka," he said, looking deeply into her eyes. "You will have an education here in Canada. No one will ever tell you that you are not good enough. It's hard for me, but not for you." Papa turned back to his dinner. Margit stared at her father.

But it's hard for me too, she cried silently. Papa didn't see that and she couldn't tell him. "I'd like to be excused," said Margit. "I still have some homework to finish for tomorrow."

"You see how seriously she takes her studies," said Papa. "She's our smart girl."

Margit left the table and went to her bedroom. Suddenly the place that had been created for her in the living room was anything but private. On the other side of the curtain, Margit could still hear her parents talking and planning for something that Papa might be able to do for work.

Margit slumped heavily onto her bed and glanced around. Mamma had tried so hard to make this space special for Margit. The curtains separating her from the rest of the family had bright pink and red flowers, set against a pale yellow background. Margit had chosen the material because it reminded her of a garden, and that's what she imagined each time she stared at it. If she closed her eyes, she could almost smell the fragrance of the flowers. It hardly even mattered that there was no window in this part of the room. The curtains provided the only window she needed.

Mamma had made a cover for Margit's feather comforter that was pale yellow and matched the yellow in the curtains. Even the pillows were covered in a matching fabric. Best of all, Margit had her own bookshelf. Someone down the road had put it out for the garbage and Mamma had rescued it. It was old and one shelf was broken. But with Mamma's help, Margit had sanded the wood and rubbed polish deep into its grain. Now the old wood shone with a soft rich lustre.

When the bookshelf was ready, Margit had filled it with her favourites: *Anne of Green Gables, Hannah of the Highlands, Little Women,* and *Through the Looking-Glass.* There was even a book about the life of Nellie McClung, a Canadian pioneer, teacher, and author. *I wonder if Nellie McClung had to learn about science when she was in school,* thought Margit.

There, in the relative safety of this private place, this "almost" room, Margit reached for her schoolbag and pulled out her science book. With a sigh, she opened it to the pages that contained pictures of the parts of the human body. *So many complicated names,* thought Margit, staring blankly at the pages. *It's impossible for me to remember all of them and to understand what each organ does.* Margit closed her eyes, trying to visualize one of the pictures, searching for the names and their meaning. It was no use. She couldn't remember.

In the living room next to Margit, Papa had turned on his record player and was singing along to an old song. Jack snuggled willingly in Papa's arm, listening as his father rocked him to sleep.

Good night, my boy, my sweet one.
Here in my arms you stay.
I wish you wisdom, my dear son,
And success will be yours one day.

Margit smiled in spite of herself. Even baby Jack was getting the message that he had better do well. With a deep sigh, Margit turned back to her books. She'd take Alice up on her offer to study together. Anything might help.

CHAPTER N.º 9

Margit approached Alice the next day before the bell rang for school. "I'm sorry, Alice," she said. "I didn't mean to get mad at you."

Alice paused at the door. "Any luck talking to your parents?"

Margit shook her head. "I didn't even try. But I know what I have to do. I just have to learn these science notes and hope I do well on the next test. That way I'll avoid Mrs. Cook *and* my parents."

Alice studied her friend a moment before replying. "I still think you're going at this the wrong way. You need to talk to your parents, not avoid them."

"No!" Margit was firm. "Trust me on this one. Talking to my parents is the last thing I want to do." She continued more gently. "Will you study with me? You're my only hope."

Alice paused and then reached out to hug Margit. "I said I'd help you. That's what friends are for."

Margit returned the hug warmly. At least she had Alice on her side.

Every afternoon for the next week, Alice returned with Margit to her apartment to study.

"Hello, Mr. Freed. I'm very happy to meet you," Alice said the first time she was introduced to Margit's father.

Margit watched Papa take Alice's hand and bow slightly in his formal European manner. "It is a pleasure," he replied. With his thick accent, it sounded as if he had said "Eeet eees a play–zure." Margit looked on, embarrassed. Papa was so different from Alice's Canadian parents. Would

Alice even understand her father? But Alice smiled and nodded.

"Your father seems very kind," she later whispered to Margit when they were inside the curtained room. "I can't believe he'd get angry with you for anything." Margit glared at Alice, warning her not to start that conversation again. Alice shrugged her shoulders and flopped onto Margit's bed.

"Okay," she said, pulling out her science book. "Let's start with some basic questions about respiration. What's in the air we breathe?" Alice drilled Margit on the parts of the lungs while Margit struggled to answer the questions. Words like *oxygenation* and *gaseous waste* left Margit completely dumbfounded.

On the last day of studying, Mamma came in with pastries and milk for the girls. "I can't let you go hungry," she said, setting down two plates with large slices of apple strudel.

"I never go hungry when I come here, Mrs. Freed," said Alice. "Your pastry is delicious."

Mamma smiled at the appreciative remark. "How is the studying coming?" she asked.

"Fine, Mamma," replied Margit, rising to push her mother out of the room.

"Ah, you are working so hard. There is no time, even for a break." Mamma smiled proudly as she left.

Margit returned to her bed. Patiently, Alice went over the science notes again and again. Margit tried to remember everything she had to know. She tried tricks to keep the information in her mind. She even tried rhymes. But nothing seemed to help. At the end of several hours, Alice looked at her watch and rose.

"I've got to go home. My parents will be expecting me." Alice sighed. "Just go over everything again before you go to sleep. Maybe it will sink in while you're dreaming."

Margit was not sure whether she knew more or less than when they had started.

That night Margit heard her father cry out again in his sleep. She sat up cautiously and pushed her comforter away. The apartment was freezing. In winter, there was never enough heat coming from the old pipes. Margit shivered from the cold and the fear creeping through her body. The moans and cries were louder now, resonating through the apartment, rising and falling with a force and power that was overwhelming. As Margit approached the door to the bedroom, she heard the cries turn into words.

"Stop, stop, stop!" Papa wailed. "Don't hurt me. No, please! How can I live? Please, stop!" Margit paused, paralyzed by the agonizing sound coming from her father. The pain in his voice was intense and unbearable.

"*Shah*, Leo." Margit heard the voice of her mother, struggling to comfort Papa. "It's a dream, a nightmare. *Shah*. You must be quiet. You must wake up. You'll wake the children. Leo, you're here with me. You're not in Europe. The war is over. You're safe."

Margit listened as Papa's moans turned to whimpers and then to silence. The nightmare was over. Shaking, Margit quietly returned to her bed and dove under the covers. Her mind was spinning. Physically, Papa was slowly regaining his strength, eating more, gaining weight, and walking with more assurance. But inside, the pain had travelled with him to Canada like extra baggage, so heavy it weighed him down. How long before Papa's suffering would end? It was so unfair that here in Canada he couldn't even find a job. She just had to do well on her test. She had to please her parents. Under no circumstances could she cause her father more pain. Margit tried in vain to get back to sleep, but she simply could not settle. When morning came, she was exhausted.

CHAPTER N⁰ 10

Margit was one of the last students to slide into her chair the next day. Mrs. Cook gave her a stern look as she passed out the test papers. "No talking, class. You'll have one hour to complete the test. Good luck."

Margit buried her head in the test paper. It seemed like only seconds had passed when Mrs. Cook spoke again. "That's it, class. Please hand in your papers and then take out your history books."

The rest of the day passed in a blur. Margit could barely concentrate on anything that

Mrs. Cook was saying. Her mind buzzed with science facts and figures and the strain of trying to figure out how she had done on the test. When the day ended, Margit flew out the door, past Alice, who tried to catch up with her. Margit did not have the energy to talk to anyone. All she wanted was to get home and flop on her bed, close her eyes, and block out the events of the day.

"Margitka," a familiar voice called to her as she bolted down the stairs of the school building.

"Papa? What are you doing here?" Margit's father stood at the bottom of the stairs, holding onto his wool cap as it threatened to fly off his head in the fierce wind.

"Your Mamma needed things from the market, but she was too busy with her sewing to go. I hoped you would come with me."

Margit sighed. Papa stood with such expectation on his face. Margit did not have the heart to tell him that she was simply not in the mood for company. Instead, she took her father's arm and steered him in the direction of Kensington Market. "Of course I'll come with you, Papa."

All the way to the market, Papa tried to talk to his daughter, but Margit's head was still filled with science questions. *Maybe, just maybe, I answered enough questions correctly to pass,* Margit thought and prayed.

Papa paused outside the butcher shop to watch an ancient-looking woman with a shawl on her head clean feathers from a chicken. Deftly, she plucked and scraped until the carcass was clean. Then the chicken was tossed onto a mound of ice already laden with chicken pieces, while the woman reached for another slaughtered bird to clean. She moved with the precision and speed of a surgeon.

"We need to get some meat," said Papa under his breath, reaching into his pocket for his wallet. "But I'm not sure I have enough money. It won't be easy until I find work."

Margit winced. *Papa has to find a job soon,* she thought.

"Margit!" Margit looked up to see Alice waving and calling to her from across the road. Her heart sank. She didn't want to see Alice— didn't want Alice to say anything about school. Frantically, she tried to steer her father inside the butcher shop and away from her friend. But it was too late.

"Hello, Mr. Freed. Hi, Margit." Alice's face was red from the sprint across the street. "You ran off after school and I didn't get a chance to speak to you."

Margit quickly jumped in before Alice could say another word. "I had to shop with my father. And we've got a lot to do. And my mother is waiting at home for us."

Alice wasn't listening to her. "Come into our flower shop. I want my parents to meet your father. I've told them all about him."

Before Margit could object further, her father had taken Alice by the arm and followed her across the road and into her parents' store. Margit ran to catch up with them.

"This is Mr. Freed," said Alice, introducing Papa to her parents. "Remember? I told you all about him."

"We're so very happy you're here in Canada," said Mrs. Donald.

Papa took off his cap and bowed low, taking Mrs. Donald's hand. "I am honoured," he replied. "We buy food for home," continued Papa, stumbling over the English.

Margit cringed. Her father looked so different from Alice's parents, so formal, so foreign. But Mr. and Mrs. Donald hardly seemed to notice.

"Your father is charming, Margit," said Mrs. Donald. "So refined. Such a gentleman. Now, I think that Mrs. Freed would love some flowers to go on her table, don't you agree Mr. Freed?" With that, she turned her back and began to select a bouquet of red roses and white lilies. Papa stepped forward, a look of concern on his face.

"No, please," Papa said urgently, looking to Margit for help. "Flowers—nice. But … we have little money." The way he spoke, it sounded as if he had said, "lee–tell moan–ee." Margit was horrified. She was embarrassed about her father, who appeared so different, and ashamed that they could not afford the flowers. In that moment, she wished the floor would open up and swallow her whole.

"My father is looking for work," she interjected. "You know, he was a great lawyer in Czechoslovakia—very well known." Desperately, she tried to make her father sound important. But her humiliation was apparent. In the end, it sounded as if she were apologizing for him. Papa glanced at her and was silent. At once, Margit knew she had made things worse, drawn even more attention to her father's difference. She stopped and hung her head.

"You don't need to explain things for your father, Margit," said Mrs. Donald sternly. She turned back to Papa. "These flowers are a gift, Mr. Freed. Every table should have flowers to make it beautiful. Please give my best wishes to your wife."

Papa and Margit walked home in silence. There was a part of Margit that wished her father were like the other fathers she saw on the streets of Toronto—men in suits who went to work and spoke English with no strange accent. Guiltily, she shook her head. How could she think that way after everything Papa had been through?

At home, Mamma noted the looks on the faces of her husband and daughter but said nothing. She was pleased to accept the flowers from Papa and arranged them quickly in a vase for the table.

"There was a call today from the man at the Law Society—Mr. McIntyre." Papa nodded with recognition as Mamma continued. "He'd like you to come to see him."

"I wonder what he wants?" mused Papa. "Probably more requirements that I must fulfill to work here." He looked even more dejected than before. "Margit, you'll have to come with me tomorrow after school. I'll need your help again with the translation."

*Margit was horrified. She was
embarrassed about her father,
who appeared so different,
and ashamed that they
could not afford the flowers.*

There was little warmth in Papa's voice, and Margit was stung. She didn't want to have to accompany her father back to Osgoode Hall. She needed some time to herself—time to sort out everything she was thinking and feeling. But that was not to be the case.

"Of course, Papa," she replied. "I'll meet you outside when school is finished."

Papa was waiting for Margit the next day
after school. Margit tried hard not to notice the
tension that was still in the air between them. She
wanted to throw her arms around his neck, to
make him forget how she had shamed him the
previous day. But she didn't. Instead, she took
Papa's arm and together they made their way
back to Osgoode Hall and the Law Society.

Mr. McIntyre stood up behind his desk when
they were finally shown into his office. "Ah,
Mr. Freed," he said warmly. "I'm happy to see
you again. Please have a seat."

Margit and her father sat down and waited politely for Mr. McIntyre to continue speaking.

"I must tell you that I feel terrible about our last meeting," he began. "I can only imagine how difficult things must be for you. And how different things are here in Canada." He waited patiently for Margit to explain his words to her father. Margit stumbled slightly on the translation. Wherever she went, she was reminded of Papa's differences.

"But after you left my office the last time, I remembered something." He paused and leaned forward. "I know about a job you might be interested in," he said and smiled. "You won't be working as a lawyer, but it is work, and it is a good job. Take this note from me and it will get you an interview." He pushed a piece of paper into Papa's hands.

Papa took the paper gently, as if it might break if handled roughly. His eyes shone and he could barely speak. After what seemed like an eternity, he stood and grabbed Mr. McIntyre's hand, shaking it fiercely.

"I am grateful," he finally blurted out.

Mr. McIntyre stood and returned the handshake warmly. "Good luck," Mr. McIntyre said and then turned to Margit. "I know it's been almost impossible for immigrants to get into Canada, especially Jews like your father. Our country has a lot to be proud of when it comes to this past war. Our soldiers served us well overseas. But I for one am not proud of having turned our backs on so many Jewish people during this terrible time. And now our country is still so afraid of strangers, afraid they will take jobs away from those who were born here. Well, I don't believe that for a minute. Tell your father that I admire all of you who managed to survive in Europe."

With that, Mr. McIntyre sat back down and resumed his work. Margit and Papa turned and left the office. It was only after they had descended the stairs of Osgoode Hall that Papa was finally able to speak fully.

Papa was jubilant as he looked at his daughter. "Your Mamma was right," he said. "Things will get better and better. *A bis'l libe un a bisele glick.* A little bit of love and a little bit of luck. That's what we have, Margit." The tension between them was suddenly forgotten. Determination was written all over his face. "Come. It's time to find work."

Margit directed her father to the corner of Chestnut and Albert streets, close to Osgoode Hall. There across the street was Hillock's Lumberyard. The sign in front said, "Help wanted. Apply within." It was like a beacon, a guiding light of encouragement that had appeared when they most needed it.

Margit pushed open the door marked "Office" and, still holding her father's arm, entered the dimly lit room. Three large wooden desks were lined up in a row, like the desks in her classroom, only much bigger. They were piled high with papers, binders, and books, like little mountains of official procedures. Wooden filing cabinets lined the wall, each one sagging under the weight of more books and papers. Light filtered in through one dirty glass window and mingled with the light from the naked light bulb hanging from the ceiling. Display boards containing wood samples—pine, walnut, and oak, each cut to reveal its own special grain—provided the only artwork on the walls.

"Can I help you?" An anxious-looking man peered out from behind a pile of paperwork and stared at Margit and her father.

Papa nudged Margit forward. "Yes, please. My name is Margit Freed and this is my father, Leo Freed." Margit launched into her well-rehearsed and familiar speech. "My father would like to inquire about work. Mr. McIntyre from the Law Society said we should come here."

The man eyed Margit and her father carefully. "Does your father talk?" he asked. A small smile was forming at the corner of his lips.

Papa raised his head and stepped forward. "Of course," he said. "My English is poor ... but I learn."

The man paused again. "I'm Mr. Hillock. My bookkeeper quit a month ago and I've been looking for a new one ever since—someone who can take care of my accounts and clear up some of this mess." His arm swept impatiently around the room. "I've got order numbers and bank numbers and payment numbers, and no one to help sort it out." He looked over at Papa. "Mr. Freed, is it?"

Margit spoke briefly to her father and then turned back to Mr. Hillock. "My father is an educated man. He was a lawyer back home. He knows about business." Margit held her breath as Mr. Hillock continued to inspect the two of them.

"Numbers are the same ... in Czech and in English," interrupted Papa.

Mr. Hillock smiled broadly. "Well, sir, you're right about that! When can you start?"

Papa stared, almost speechless. He pumped Mr. Hillock's hand. "I start tomorrow. I work hard for you. You see!"

Papa and Margit left Mr. Hillock's office, emerging into the cold dim light of the end of the day.

Papa grabbed Margit, dancing crazily with her in the middle of the street. Margit danced along. She didn't care how silly they looked. She only cared about her father's happiness. *Yes,* she thought. *Everything was going to be fine.*

"A bis'l libe un a bisele glick," sang Papa in a loud voice. "A little bit of love and a little bit of luck. I knew it, Margit. I knew something would happen. I have work and that's good. It's not the work I used to do. But today, any kind of work is good." Papa squeezed Margit with a strength she didn't know he had. Then he pulled away and looked deeply into her eyes. "Getting a good education in Canada," he said. "That's what's important. Do well in school, Margit. That is all I ask. It's the only gift you can give me. Do well and you can do and be whatever you want!"

Papa continued to dance and sing as he waltzed up the street with his daughter close behind. In his joy, Papa didn't even notice the look on Margit's face.

CHAPTER N.º 12

Margit was distracted all the way home from the lumberyard. On the one hand, she was happy that Papa had found work, relieved to see the joy in his eyes that, hours earlier, had been so sad. On the other hand, she was still troubled by his belief that she was doing so well in school, and by the secret that she was hiding about her work in science. How could she ever measure up to what her parents expected of her? This was so unfair, Margit thought. After all, she herself had not been in Canada for that long, and she was trying so hard to do well. Doing well just didn't seem to be enough for her parents. They wanted her to do extraordinarily well—better than anyone else.

Margit wanted so badly to talk to her father, to explain her situation to him, to try to make him understand that she wasn't the perfect student he thought she was. But listening to his speech about succeeding made her believe that Papa simply would not understand. So, she said nothing.

Papa, for his part, didn't even notice. All the way home on the streetcar, he hummed and whistled songs and tapped lightly on his knee.

In the field, flowers grow,
Over mountains, breezes blow.
Oh, what joy we have, singing a song.
Laughter and joy, all day long.

"Your Mamma will be so pleased," Papa said. "I can tell you, Margit, that I didn't always think I'd be able to get work. But your Mamma said

I would find something. And she was right." He didn't wait for a response. "Maybe, if things go well at Hillock's, I'll even go back to school. Anything is possible, Margit. Didn't I tell you that? Anything is possible!"

Margit sighed deeply. At that moment, nothing seemed possible to her.

By the time Margit and her father arrived at home, it was dark, and Margit was tired and hungry. She couldn't wait to eat a quick dinner and then retreat to the privacy of her bedroom space. But once again, that was not to be the case. Walking up the stairs of their building, Margit could hear voices coming from their apartment.

"I wonder who's here?" she said, turning the knob to their apartment and entering curiously. Mamma was there, seated on the couch, and Jack played quietly on the floor. Then, as Margit's eyes swept the room, her heart sank and her hands began to tremble.

"Hello, Margit." Mrs. Cook looked evenly in her direction, peering over her dark glasses. Her expression was cool and serious. In her hands, she held an open folder with papers and worksheets. Without looking closely, Margit knew immediately that it was a collection of her science papers and assignments. And on top was the science test she had just completed. The letter D stood out once again, glowing in the dim light of the living-room lamp.

Mamma looked up at her husband and Margit. "Leo," she began. "This is Mrs. Cook, Margit's teacher." Mamma looked bewildered as Papa entered the living room and shook hands with Mrs. Cook. "Margit," Mamma continued. "Mrs. Cook is here to talk about your grades. You never said a word, Margit. I don't understand what has happened."

"Let me explain for the sake of your husband," interrupted Mrs. Cook. "Mr. Freed, I'm afraid your daughter is doing very poorly in science. I have been concerned for some time and I have tried to get your wife to call me. But it seems Margit failed to pass that message along."

Mrs. Cook stared hard at Margit, as did Mamma and Papa. Silence filled the room. Even Jack stopped playing and looked intently at the adults. Margit wilted under their gazes. The truth was out in the open now, and Margit could not longer hide from it.

"I'm sorry, Mamma, Papa," she stammered. "I didn't want to worry you. I didn't want to disappoint you. I know it's been so hard with Papa. And I know you expect me to do so well. And I just couldn't tell you how hard this has been." Margit hung her head low. There was nothing else to say. Not only had she fallen short in science, but she had also failed her parents, and that was the worst realization of all.

Minutes passed. Finally, Papa turned to Mrs. Cook and with Mamma's help began to talk about Margit's schoolwork. They reviewed her science tests and then talked about her work in all her school subjects. Margit sank into a chair, barely listening to what was being said. Her head pounded as the noises blended into one big distorted sound. After what seemed like an eternity, Mrs. Cook stood to leave.

"I'll see you tomorrow in class, Margit." She continued to peer at Margit over her glasses. "Don't be late. Goodbye, Mrs. Freed, Mr. Freed. I think this meeting has been very productive."

The door closed behind Mrs. Cook, leaving Margit to face her parents.

Still Margit sat, with her head low, unable to look up. She closed her eyes and squeezed them tight, trying to shut out the moment, wishing she were anywhere but here in the room with her parents staring down at her. Papa was the first one to break the silence.

"I'm so unhappy, so disappointed, Margit," he said so softly she had to strain to hear him.

It was worse than if he had shouted out loud at her.

"I'm sorry I'm such a failure, Papa," Margit said finally as she looked up at her parents. Her voice quivered and tears threatened to spill from her eyes. "I know that doing well in school is more important than anything else in the world."

"No," said Papa. "You don't understand. I'm so unhappy that you couldn't come to me and tell me about your difficulties."

"But I thought you'd be so angry with me!" cried Margit.

Mamma stepped forward and placed her hand gently on Margit's shoulder. "How could you possibly think we wouldn't understand, Margit?"

Tears poured from Margit's eyes. Frantically she wiped them away. "All those things you said about an education, about doing well, about succeeding. What else could I think?"

"Of course it's important to do well," continued Papa. "But Margit, you do well in so many things. You don't have to do well in everything.

And as for what is more important than anything else in the world to me, well, that's simple. It's you, Margitka. You and Mamma and Jack. Nothing is more important than that."

Margit sat back, astonished. How wrong she had been! She had misjudged her parents completely. Alice had been right all along. Suddenly the weight of having to carry her secret was lifted and she felt light and relieved.

"I've been wrong," said Papa. "I was thinking too much about myself and never saw that you were troubled. I want you to believe that you can always come and talk to your Mamma and to me, especially if there is a problem. Do you promise?"

Margit nodded.

"*A bis'l libe un a bisele glick,*" said Papa.

"I know," replied Margit. "A little bit of love and a little bit of luck."

"We need them both," said Mamma.

"We have them both," replied Papa. And he proceeded to tell her the news about his job. Mamma was overjoyed. Jack clapped his hands

"*I know,*" *replied Margit.*
"*A little bit of love and a little
bit of luck.*"
"*We have them both,*"
replied Papa.

and shouted out loud, as if he too understood everything that was being said and wanted in on the conversation.

"I'll need your help, Margit," continued Papa. "You're the one who is good at English. Perhaps I can help you with science if you'll help your Papa learn to speak English like a real Canadian. I could use some help fitting in."

"You don't have to be like everyone else, Papa," replied Margit.

ACKNOWLEDGMENTS

MANY THANKS TO BARBARA BERSON FOR HER LEADERSHIP AND
GUIDANCE IN THE ONGOING DEVELOPMENT OF THIS SERIES OF
STORIES ABOUT MARGIT. THANKS ALSO TO CATHERINE DORTON
FOR HER CREATIVITY AND ATTENTIVENESS TO THE STORY.
I AM ALSO GRATEFUL TO DAWN HUNTER FOR HER THOROUGH
EDITING OF THE BOOK. IT HAS BEEN A PLEASURE TO WORK
WITH THE ENTIRE CREATIVE TEAM AT PENGUIN, AND
I CONTINUE TO BE GRATEFUL FOR BEING INCLUDED
IN THE OUR CANADIAN GIRL PROJECT.

THANKS, AS ALWAYS, TO MY FAMILY AND FRIENDS, ESPECIALLY
MY HUSBAND, IAN EPSTEIN, AND MY CHILDREN, GABI AND
JAKE. I CHERISH THEIR LOVE AND SUPPORT.

Dear Reader,

*Welcome back to the continuing adventures of
Our Canadian Girl! It's been another exciting
year for us here at Penguin, publishing new stories
and continuing the adventures of twelve terrific
girls. The best part of this past year, though, has
been the wonderful letters we've received from
readers like you, telling us about your favourite
Our Canadian Girl story, and the parts you
liked the most. Best of all, you told us which
stories you would like to read, and we were
amazed! There are so many remarkable stories
in Canadian history. It seems that wherever we
live, great stories live too, in our towns and cities,
on our rivers and mountains. Thank you so much
for sharing them.*

*So please, stay in touch. Write letters, log on to
our website (www.ourcanadiangirl.ca), let us
know what you think of Our Canadian Girl.
We're listening.*

Sincerely,
  Barbara Berson

Canada's

1608
Samuel de
Champlain
establishes
the first
fortified
trading post
at Quebec.

1759
The British
defeat the
French in
the Battle
of the
Plains of
Abraham.

1812
The United
States
declares war
against
Canada.

1845
The expedition of
Sir John Franklin
to the Arctic ends
when the ship is
frozen in the pack
ice; the fate of its
crew remains a
mystery.

1869
Louis Riel
leads his
Métis
followers in
the Red
River
Rebellion.

1871
British
Columbia
joins
Canada.

1755
The British
expel the
entire French
population
of Acadia
(today's
Maritime
provinces),
sending
them into
exile.

1776
The 13
Colonies
revolt
against
Britain, and
the Loyalists
flee to
Canada.

1837
Calling for
responsible
government, the
Patriotes, following
Louis-Joseph
Papineau, rebel in
Lower Canada;
William Lyon
Mackenzie leads the
uprising in Upper
Canada.

1867
New
Brunswick,
Nova Scotia
and the United
Province of
Canada come
together in
Confederation
to form the
Dominion of
Canada.

1870
Manitoba joins
Canada. The
Northwest
Territories
become an
official
territory of
Canada.

1762
Elizabeth

1862
Lisa